THE LOYAL CAT

BROWNDEER PRESS

HARCOURT BRACE & COMPANY

SAN DIEGO   NEW YORK   LONDON

PRINTED IN SINGAPORE

THE
LOYAL
CAT

RETOLD BY

LENSEY NAMIOKA

ILLUSTRATED BY

AKI SOGABE

Browndeer Press is a registered trademark of Harcourt Brace & Company.

Library of Congress Cataloging-in-Publication Data
Namioka, Lensey.
The loyal cat/by Lensey Namioka; illustrated by Aki Sogabe.
p.   cm.
"Browndeer Press."
Summary: In ancient Japan, a loyal cat uses his magic powers to
help his friend, a poor and humble priest.
ISBN 0-15-200092-5
[1. Fairy tales. 2. Cats — Fiction. 3. Magic — Fiction. 4. Japan —
Fiction.] I. Sogabe, Aki, ill. II. Title.
PZ8.N123Lo   1995
[E] — dc20   94-10937

First edition
A B C D E

Each picture in this book was made from a single sheet of black paper, cut freehand
and placed over rice papers that were colored using airbrush or watercolor.
The display type was set in Herculanum.
The text type was set in Centaur by Thompson Type, San Diego, California.
Color separations were made by Bright Arts, Ltd., Singapore.
Printed and bound by Tien Wah Press, Singapore
This book was printed with soya-based inks on Leykam recycled paper,
which contains more than 20 percent postconsumer waste and has
a total recycled content of at least 50 percent.
Production supervision by Warren Wallerstein and Ginger Boyer
Designed by Lisa Peters

Deep in the mountains of northern Japan is a small temple called Hukuzo-ji. It is known as the Cat Temple. This is how the temple got its name.

About three hundred and seventy years ago, there lived at Hukuzo-ji a priest called Tetsuzan. He was a very holy man. He knew thousands of prayers by heart, more than any other priest in the region. It would have taken him almost a week to recite them all.

The priests at other temples had big, round voices. When they wore their silk robes and recited their prayers, they looked impressive and sounded important. Their temples always had many visitors who gave rich gifts of gold, silks, and valuable art.

But Tetsuzan was a gentle person with a soft voice. He didn't care about sounding important. Few people came to his temple with gifts.

No fine paintings hung on the walls of his temple; no flowers decorated the altar. The food he ate was plain, and the clothes he wore were made

of cotton. Tetsuzan didn't need much money because he enjoyed simple things. He liked to water the moss in the garden and sweep the pine needles from the steps.

One day, when Tetsuzan was in his garden, he heard a pitiful mewing sound above his head. He looked up. Some monkeys in a tree had seized a kitten and were cruelly teasing it. Tetsuzan frightened the monkeys away. He took the kitten inside and gently stroked it.

When the kitten got over its fright, it said, "Thank you for saving me. I will never forget what you have done."

The kitten was called Huku, and from that time on he lived in the temple and became Tetsuzan's loyal friend. As Huku grew older, he discovered that he had magical powers. He was able to raise objects into the air and keep them there as long as he wanted. But, being a cat, he kept his powers a secret.

Now, because few people gave his temple gifts, Tetsuzan grew poorer and poorer. He could no longer feed his monks, and so they left. Only Huku stayed.

Tetsuzan became too poor to fix the torn paper in his windows, and when the wind blew, the torn flaps whistled. The mats on the floor were old and rotted.

Once when Tetsuzan was eating his bowl of thin yam soup, he saw Huku looking hungrily at him. "Didn't you catch any mice today?" he asked.

Huku looked down and sadly licked his paws. "There's so little food left to steal that the last mouse has gone," he said.

Tetsuzan felt sorry for Huku. Although he himself was a vegetarian, he went into the village and begged for fish heads and tails for his loyal cat.

One day, a young country girl called Osen came to see Tetsuzan. She had lived near the temple and now worked as a maid at the lord's castle. As she sat and played with Huku, she told Tetsuzan some news.

"The old lord of the castle has just died," she said. "His son, the young lord, is planning a magnificent funeral. He wants everybody to think that

he is a great man, even greater than his father."

"You must be working hard to prepare for the event," said Tetsuzan.

"That's true," said Osen. "I'd better hurry. Many important priests have been invited to pray at the funeral."

After the maid left, Huku looked thoughtfully at Tetsuzan. "You know more prayers than anyone else. You are a holy man. You should have been invited to the funeral."

"All the famous priests will be there," said Tetsuzan. "They won't want me."

"We'll see about that," purred Huku to himself. He put his head down on his paws and began to think. How could he use his magical powers to help his friend?

The cat knew that if Tetsuzan prayed at the funeral of the old lord, people would see what a good man he was. They would honor him. They would flock to his temple and bring gifts. Tetsuzan would be able to wear silk robes. And Huku would have plenty to eat.

After thinking all night, Huku had an idea. He set out that very morning for the castle.

The castle of the young lord was nearby, and Huku arrived just as the funeral service started. The friends, relatives, and followers of the old lord were all there, curious to see the young lord and compare him with his father.

The funeral service was held in a big reception hall of the castle. Huku saw hundreds of people listening to the beautiful voice of a famous priest reciting a prayer.

The air was heavy with the smell of incense. The embroidered silk robes of the priest glittered brightly. The only sounds were the priest's beautiful voice and every now and then a soft *bong* as he tapped a bronze bowl with a stick.

Huku looked around. At one end of the reception hall there was an alcove with a low shelf, and on the shelf was a beautiful bowl of flowers. It had been placed there by the young lord's wife, who was especially proud of her skill in flower arranging.

Huku went to work. He stared at the alcove. Slowly the bowl of flowers rose into the air until it floated two feet above the shelf.

The young lord's wife was horrified when she saw her beautiful flower arrangement floating in the air. "Something strange is happening!" she whispered to her husband.

The young lord turned away impatiently. "Don't bother me now. Can't you see that we have important guests here?"

Huku was disappointed. He decided to try something different.

A painting hung in the alcove — a famous picture usually kept in storage. The precious work had been taken out, unrolled, and displayed in honor of the occasion.

Huku stared hard at the painting. Slowly the bottom of the painting rolled up, until half the picture was hidden.

An attendant rushed over and tried to pull the scroll down. But it wouldn't unroll.

"My lady, look at the painting!" she whispered to the young lord's wife.

The young lord's wife gasped. "You must look!" she whispered to her husband. "Something *really* strange is happening!"

"Didn't I tell you not to bother me?" said the young lord.

Again Huku was disappointed. "I have to do something more drastic," he said to himself.

But before he could think of anything else, the service ended and everyone got up to follow the coffin of the old lord that was being carried to the cemetery. There was a long procession.

Huku knew what he had to do. It would be hard work, but this time the young lord would have to pay attention.

Huku stared hard at the coffin, which was in a cart at the head of the procession. Slowly the coffin rose up from the cart. It rose higher and higher until it was fifteen feet in the air. "You stay there until I'm ready to let you down," Huku said to the coffin.

When they saw the floating coffin, all the people in the procession began to shout and scream.

This was something the young lord could no longer ignore. What was his father's coffin doing up in the air? It was disgraceful! It was undignified! It was embarrassing!

"Send me ten of my strongest warriors!" ordered the young lord.

The warriors came and threw ropes over the coffin. They pulled and they pulled. They gnashed their teeth, they rolled their eyes, and they pulled with all their might. But they couldn't pull the coffin down.

Huku purred and stroked his whiskers as he watched from the end of the procession.

The young lord stared at his warriors in disgust. "Bring me my ten strongest wrestlers!" he ordered.

The wrestlers were all huge men. They pulled and they pulled. Their muscles rippled, and the sweat poured down their backs in little streams. But they couldn't pull the coffin down.

Huku washed his face.

Then one of the priests stepped up. "My lord, it must have been a magic spell that raised the coffin," he said. "I will recite a prayer to break the spell."

The young lord nodded, and the priest began to pray in his loud and beautiful voice. But the coffin remained in the air. One by one, all the other famous priests recited prayers. Still, the coffin refused to come down.

The young lord was frantic. "I will offer a fine reward to the man who can bring down my father's coffin!" he cried.

Huku saw Osen standing with the other serving women at the end of
the procession. He went up to her and rubbed against her ankles.

Osen looked down and recognized the cat. She thought of Tetsuzan.

Osen rushed up to the young lord and said, "My lord, there is a very
holy priest called Tetsuzan from a small temple nearby. He knows many,
many prayers. Perhaps he can help you."

The young lord had no choice. "Very well, send for him," he said.

When Tetsuzan arrived, everyone was surprised to see a modest-looking man dressed in a tattered cotton robe. Could such a man succeed, when all those famous priests had failed?

Tetsuzan began to pray, and the crowd grew quiet. As soon as Huku heard his friend, he released the coffin. Slowly — very, *very* slowly — the coffin descended. It landed on the ground with only a gentle thump. The crowd sighed.

The young lord was so relieved he almost wept. "Tell me what you want for your reward," he said to Tetsuzan. "I will give you as much gold as you wish."

Tetsuzan had no idea what to say. He looked around and saw Huku at the back of the crowd. This was the moment the cat had hoped for. He raised his front paw and held up three toes.

Three toes? Ah, thought Tetsuzan, I understand. "I should like three pieces of gold," he said.

The young lord was surprised. He had been prepared to give a great deal more. What a modest man this holy priest was!

The young lord summoned his treasurer and ordered the gold to be placed in a beautiful lacquered box. As Tetsuzan received his reward, everyone sighed again. The young lord's wife wiped away a tear.

Huku quietly let down the bowl of flowers and unrolled the picture.
Then he and Tetsuzan made their way home.

"Let's see your reward," Huku said eagerly, when they were back at the temple.

Tetsuzan opened the box and showed Huku the three gold pieces.

When the cat saw the gold pieces, his back arched. "You asked for only three gold pieces?" he hissed.

"But . . . but you held up three toes of your paw," stammered Tetsuzan.

"I held up three toes because I wanted you to ask for *three hundred* gold pieces!" said Huku. He had wanted enough gold to make their temple rich and famous. He was very disappointed.

But Huku got over his anger. At least he and Tetsuzan had enough money to make repairs.

They bought clean white paper to mend the windows. They put in fresh, sweet-smelling mats on the floor. They had enough money for food. The monks and the mice came back. Huku became a mouser again, and soon he grew fat and sleek.

Hukuzo-ji remained a small temple deep in the mountains. Tetsuzan softly recited his prayers, watered the moss in the garden, and swept the pine needles from the steps.

Finally Huku understood that his friend preferred his quiet life. He
would not have been happy as the priest of a big, famous temple.

But once in a while, when Huku thought about the three hundred pieces of gold, his eyes flashed green fire.

When people heard the story of the cat who helped his master, they began to call Hukuzo-ji the Cat Temple.

Today, you can visit the Cat Temple in northern Japan. On a hill behind the temple is a stone marker in honor of Huku, the loyal cat.